CAPTAIN DUCK

*D*uck drove into my life one morning, smashed into a rock and ever since I haven't been able to get rid of him. Not that I'd really want to. Duck is always getting into some sort of trouble. Do you know what he's been up to now – hi-jacking Goat's boat, that's what. We all knew it would end in disaster, Frog, Sheep and me, but could we stop him pulling that cord to start the engine? What do you think?

Jez

For Dad with love

First published in hardback in Great Britain by HarperCollins Publishers Ltd in 2002
First published in paperback by Collins Picture Books in 2003

3 5 7 9 10 8 6 4
ISBN: 0-00-713011-2

Collins Picture Books is an imprint of the Children's Division, part of HarperCollins Publishers Ltd.
Text and illustrations copyright © Jez Alborough 2002

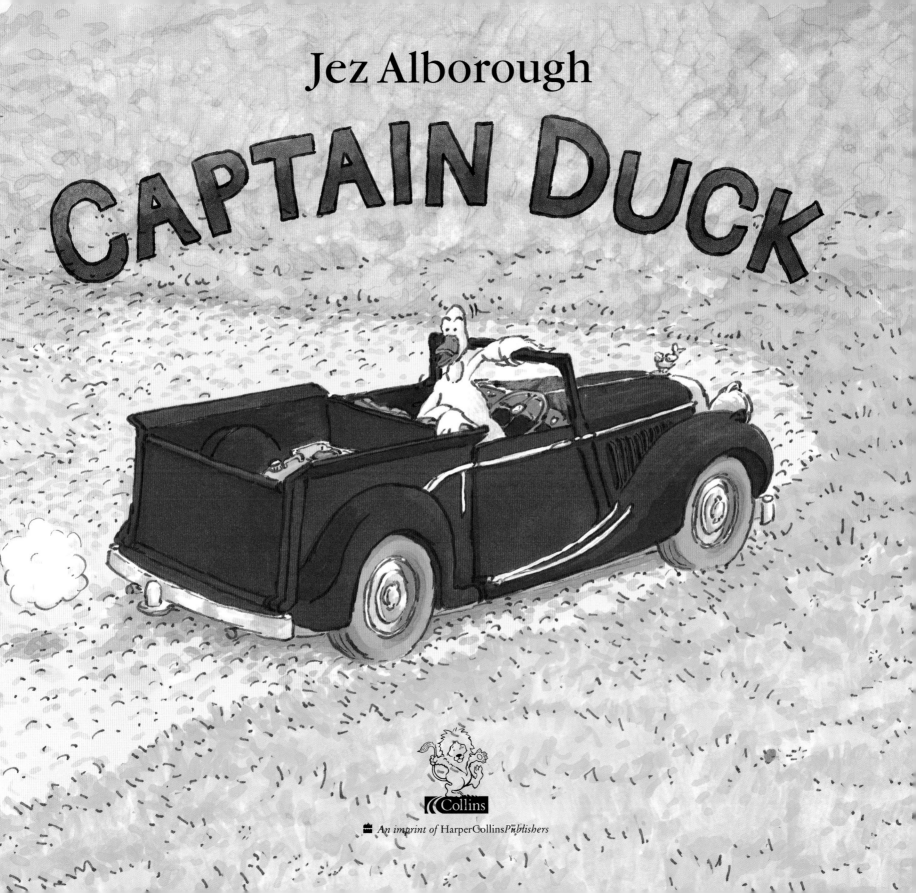

Jez Alborough

CAPTAIN DUCK

Collins

An imprint of HarperCollinsPublishers

Pop, pop, coughs the spluttering truck.
'No more petrol left,' quacks Duck.

'It's good I stopped
near my friend Goat

he uses petrol
in his boat.'

Duck rap-tap-taps at Goat's back door,
waits a while, then taps once more.

Still no answer, so instead,

he sneaks a peek inside Goat's shed.

'Hooray!' cries Duck. 'A stroke of luck –

petrol for my
thirsty truck.

I'll only take a drop or two...
Look, there's Frog! Where's he off to?'

He's off to take a trip on a boat.
'Hello!' calls Sheep. 'Hop in!' says Goat.

'There's one last thing I need to bring…
Now while I'm gone, don't pull that string.'

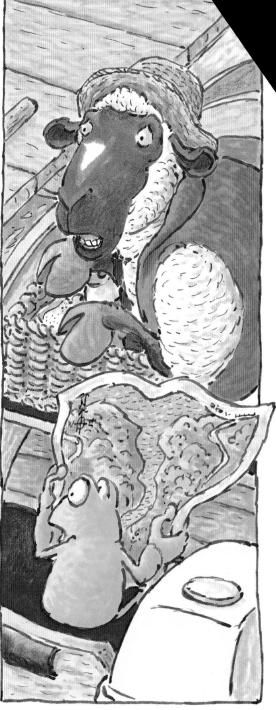

They check the map
and pack the snack.

Then suddenly,
they hear a quack.

'Ahoy there, sailors!' comes a cry.

'Is this a boating trip I spy?

If there are seas to be explored,

make way… CAPTAIN DUCK'S ON BOARD!

Let's get going!
What's this thing?'

'No!' cries Frog.
    'Don't pull that string!'

The engine roars, Frog gives a shout.
'Oh, no!' screams Sheep. 'Frog's fallen out!'

'Grab that rope,' says Duck. 'I'll steer.
Throw it out when we get near.

Ready…steady…get set…THROW!
Catch!' yells Duck. 'And here we go.

PLOP

I didn't know Frog could water-ski?'

'No,' bleats Sheep, 'and nor did he.

Oh, please, Duck. Please don't go too far.

Goat will wonder where we are.
I think you'd better stop it now…'

'I can't,' yells Duck. 'I don't know how.   Besides we've

only just begun…

and Frog is having so much fun.'

So Captain Duck steers the boat   far away from poor old Goat

who finds his can beside a truck.

'Aha!' he says. 'That naughty Duck.'

The little boat bobs on and on

until the river banks are gone.

Just then the engine
pop-pop-pops

and with a final cough
it stops.

The stormy waves begin to swell.
Sheep says, 'I don't feel too well.'

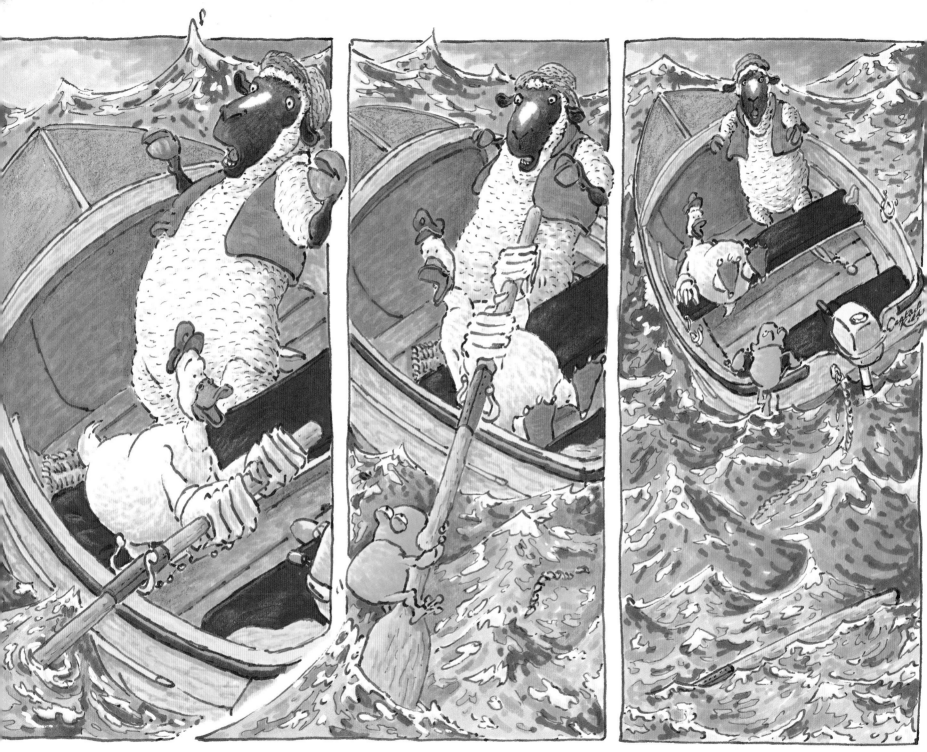

'Come on,' says Duck, 'we'll row to shore.'

'We can't,' gasps Frog.

'There's just one oar.'

They huddle in the bobbing boat
and snuggle close to Sheep's warm coat.

And there upon the restless deep

three lost friends fall fast asleep.

Through the night,
hour by hour,

Goat keeps lookout
from his tower.

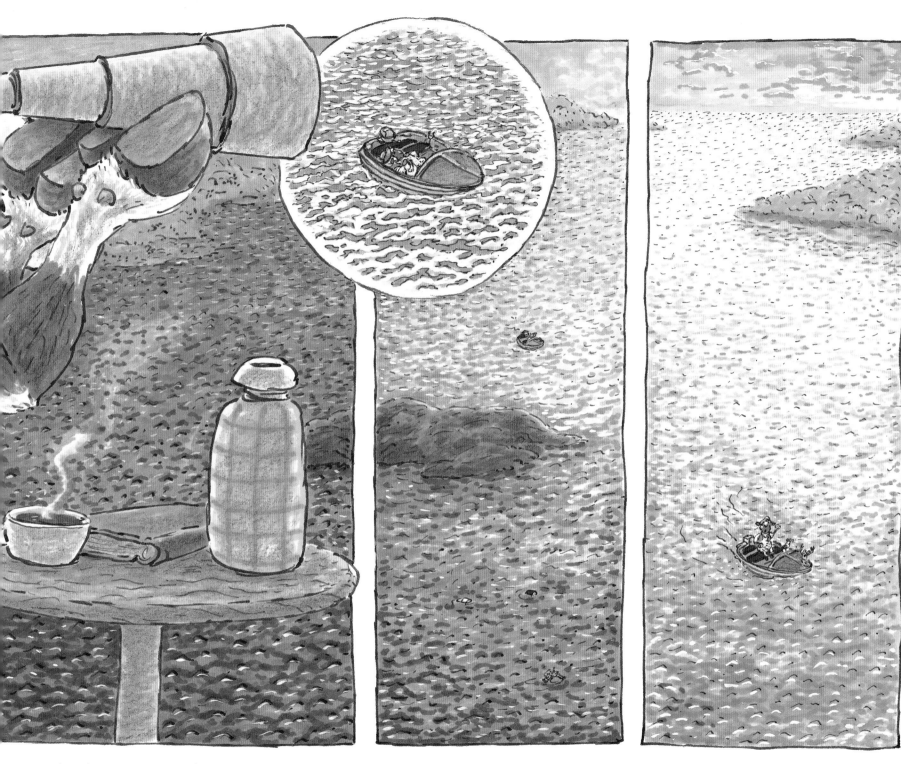

And then at dawn,
through bleary eyes,   upon the tide,   his boat he spies.

Sheep calls out, 'We're sorry, Goat.
We left you here...   we broke your boat!'

'Broken?' says Goat as Duck tries to hide.
'Oh, no, it just needed petrol inside.

That's why I went back for the can I keep spare.
I searched through my shed but the can wasn't there.'

'Wait!' says Frog. 'Duck was holding a can
It was just before our boat trip began

So Duck took the petrol.'   'That's right,' says Goat.
'Now you know why there wasn't enough in the boat.'

Look! Duck's getting away!' Sheep cries.
No, he's not!' gloats Goat with a glint in his eyes.

'He took the petrol,
that silly Duck,

but forgot to pour it into his truck!'

Look out for more hilarious stories about Duck:

This is the tale of a duck in a truck –
a truck that was stuck in some yucky brown muck.
A sheep in a jeep and a frog in a bush
saw the truck stuck and gave it a push.
But the truck stayed stuck!
What now, can you guess?
Could a goat in a boat
get them out of this mess?

'Alborough's pictures are addictive... Duck in the Truck
is a picture book where rhyme, illustration, wit and
inventiveness combine to produce outstanding quality.'
TES Primary

A leaking roof? A window stuck?
These are jobs for FIX-IT DUCK!
He's got his tools,
he's keen – he's strong,
what can possibly go wrong?
Duck is up to his old tricks,
now who will end up in a fix?

'A rumbustious story... Great fun.' *The Bookseller*

'A jaunty delight.' *The Guardian*

Highly Commended
KATE GREENAWAY
MEDAL

Duck in the Truck - Hardback 0-00-198346-6 £10.99 Paperback 0-00-664717-0 £4.99
Fix-it Duck - Hardback 0-00-710623-8 £9.99 Paperback 0-00-710624-6 £4.99